Elaine, Mary Lewis, and the Frogs

Elaine, Mary Lewis, and the Frogs

Heidi Chang

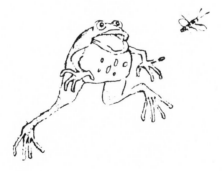

Crown Publishers, Inc.,
New York

Published by Crown Publishers, Inc., 225 Park Avenue South, New York, New
York 10003 and represented in Canada by the Canadian MANDA Group
CROWN is a trademark of Crown Publishers, Inc.
Manufactured in the United States of America

Library of Congress Cataloging-in-Publication Data
Chang, Heidi.
Elaine, Mary Lewis, and the frogs.
Summary: Chinese American Elaine Chow feels like an outcast after moving to
a small town in Iowa, until she shares a new friendship and a science project with
a girl strongly interested in frogs.
[1. Chinese Americans—Fiction.   2. Friendship—
Fiction.   3. Iowa—Fiction.   4. Frogs—Fiction]
I. Title.
PZ7.C359664El   1988   [Fic]   87-13625
ISBN 0-517-56752-0

10   9   8   7   6   5   4   3   2   1

First Edition

For Jackie, Heidi, and Patti,
the three Virgos
who taught this Pisces
how to swim.—H. C.

Chapter 1

Elaine Chow was on her way to her first day in her new school. As she walked, she thought about how much she missed her old friends and playing jump rope on the hilly streets in San Francisco. This Iowa land was so flat! Elaine put her hand inside her coat pocket and felt for

her jump rope. She always carried it, sort of for good luck. She had a feeling she would be needing good luck today!

Inside Eleanor Roosevelt Elementary School, all the kids seemed to know where they were going.

Elaine decided to ask an older girl where Classroom 312 was. "Excuse me," she said to the girl, who had a cat pin on her shirt. "Can you help me find Room 312?"

"Sure. I'm going upstairs too," the girl said. "Who is your teacher?"

"Ms. Bonovox, it says." Elaine showed the girl her registration card.

"Ms. Bonovox!" the girl exclaimed. "I had her last year."

"You did?" Elaine asked. "What's she like? I came to school last week to meet the principal, but I didn't get to meet my teacher."

"Oh, she's okay. She's just different." The girl stopped. "Here is your room. Good luck!"

Elaine smiled at the friendly girl and then turned to go into her classroom. There, at the door, was the teacher, greeting each student who came into the room. She did look a bit different. She was dressed completely in black and had big black sunglasses dangling around her neck from a long black cord. The patterns on her stockings reminded Elaine of Japanese rice crackers, with their star and triangle shapes.

Elaine handed the teacher her registration card. "Hello, Elaine," the woman said. "I'm Ms. Bonovox. Let's see, it says here you used to live in San Francisco. I used to live there, too!"

Elaine was excited. "You're from San Francisco, too?"

"Well, no. I was born and raised in New

York City. But I lived in San Francisco for a few years. Some days I really miss the sea air and pink houses. But you know, Elaine, I like it here. I hope you do too!"

I hope so, Elaine thought.

"Children, please find your desks now," said Ms. Bonovox. Elaine was in front of the room looking at the bulletin board with all the students' names on it. She quickly took a seat in the first row. A girl stood right in front of her.

"You're sitting at my desk," the girl said. Elaine was startled.

"What?" Elaine asked.

"See, the names are always on the desks the first day of school so we know where to sit. This desk says Kelleen Burke. That's me." She stared at Elaine. "You must be new here."

"Oh, I'm sorry," Elaine said. Then she felt silly. It sounded as if she were sorry for being new! Just because she didn't know the way they did things here! She looked around the room and quickly found her desk—right behind Kelleen's.

Elaine could smell the new wax on her desk. She remembered the last desk she had had in her old school. She had carved her initials in that one before she left for Iowa. Her friends Jeffrey, Kimiko, and Sherry had, too. "We'll always be friends," Elaine had said to them bravely. But now she didn't feel at all brave.

Ms. Bonovox's voice cut into Elaine's thoughts. "Class, this morning we are going to have our pictures taken for the bulletin board." Ms. Bonovox took out a camera—the kind that gives pictures instantly. "I've cut out fall leaves with your names written on them to put beneath your pictures. That way, we can all get to know each other."

After they had their pictures taken, Ms. Bonovox handed out white paper and passed around a box of colored pencils and crayons.

"I want you to draw something," Ms. Bonovox said. "Draw the most exciting thing you did this summer."

Elaine was happy. She had her own crayons—the second-largest set you could buy. She always wanted the largest set because it came with a built-in sharpener. But for some reason her mother always bought the wrong size. Elaine started a picture of her moving day. First she drew a huge truck with "Mayflower" written on the side. It stood on a big hill. Then she put herself and her cat, Mei Lee, standing next to their old house waving goodbye to Pau-Pah, Elaine's grandmother.

Elaine was so busy, she didn't notice Ms. Bonovox looking over her shoulder until her teacher said, "That's very good, Elaine." Elaine felt proud.

Kelleen turned around and wrinkled her nose at Elaine in a funny way. Elaine smiled back. But Kelleen quickly faced the front again and then leaned over to look at the paper of the boy next to her.

For a minute, Elaine got an odd feeling in her stomach. Then she saw Ms. Bonovox smile at her. It was more like half a smile, but something about it was special—it was just as if Ms. Bonovox knew what Elaine was feeling. Elaine looked down at her drawing again and let out a deep sigh.

By the time the bell rang for lunch, Elaine was almost dizzy, partly because so much new was happening and partly because she was starving. She couldn't wait to eat. Her mother had made Elaine fried rice, and since it was her first day of school, Mrs. Chow had even chopped up pieces of barbecued pork into it.

Elaine took her lunch box out of her desk and filed down to the lunchroom with the rest of the class. As she stood looking around for a place to sit, a boy ran into her with a tray. Two girls in front of Elaine were trying to see who could eat the fastest. Elaine sat down at the other end of their table. She unsnapped the fasteners on her tin lunch container.

"What's that?"

It was Kelleen. She was peering down at Elaine's lunch box.

Now Kelleen sat down. "Is that your *lunch* box? It looks like it's for carrying pencils!"

Kelleen's lunch box was bright pink plastic with kids on it who had strawberries for heads. Elaine removed the cover from her metal container.

"What's that you're eating?" Kelleen went on. "It looks like rice with little colored squares and circles."

"It is rice. It's fried rice with peas, carrots, and little pieces of barbecued pork in it," Elaine said. Hadn't Kelleen seen fried rice before?

Kelleen held out her sandwich. It was baloney. "How come you don't have a sandwich?"

"I don't know," Elaine answered. "I always have rice for lunch. Do you always have baloney sandwiches for lunch?"

"No, sometimes I have tuna, or peanut butter if my mother forgets to go to the grocery store. I'd get tired of eating baloney every day. Don't you get tired of eating rice all the time?"

"No," said Elaine, honestly. "I like rice. I have it for breakfast and dinner, too. In the morning I get rice porridge with a lot of good leftovers mixed in." Elaine smiled but Kelleen was making a face at Elaine's rice.

"Wow, I can't imagine having rice for breakfast. I usually have cereal. I like Sundays best, though, because then we have pancakes after church. Hey!" Kelleen said suddenly. "I'll give you some of my baloney sandwich if you want."

"That's okay," said Elaine. "If you're tired of baloney, do you want some of my fried rice?"

"No thank you," Kelleen said in an oddly polite way, as if she were answering a grown-up. "I think I'll trade it. There's Harry. I bet *he'll* trade. Harry!" she called, and she ran off.

Elaine looked into her lunch box. She didn't feel hungry anymore. She wished she had something to trade. She hadn't even had a chance to ask Kelleen if she liked to jump rope.

Chapter 2

The next morning, when Elaine sat down for her breakfast of rice, she stared at her bowl of *jook*—steaming rice porridge—for a long time.

"What's wrong, Elaine?" her mother asked. "You were so quiet yesterday after your first day of school, and you are quiet now, too. That's not like you!"

"Mom, why do we eat rice for breakfast instead of cereal like they do here? This one girl in class acted like she never saw anyone eating rice before!"

"We've been eating rice for years, Elaine. It didn't start with you. I ate rice growing up, and so did my mother. But you can have cereal if you like, instead."

But Elaine just finished her rice porridge.

As she walked to school, Elaine saw a few familiar faces. She smiled at some girls and boys, but it seemed as if they didn't even see her! Maybe they thought she was strange, walking all by herself and smiling. The smile froze on her face and she got a lump in her throat. It felt like the time she had gotten butterscotch candy stuck there and couldn't breathe. Or like the time her parents told her they were moving to Iowa.

She remembered that day. Her mother and father had called her into the living room to talk.

"Elaine, your father and I have something to tell you."

Right away, Elaine thought something bad

had happened. Maybe her cat had run away from home. "Did Mei Lee run away?" she asked.

"No, Elaine," Mr. Chow said. He gave his daughter a hug. "It's nothing like that. It's—we are going to move."

"Move? Where? In with Pau-Pah?" Elaine asked, confused. Pau-Pah, Elaine's grandmother, lived down the block.

"No, Elaine. We are moving far away," Mr. Chow said.

"How far? As far as cousin Hwai-Hwai lives, across the ocean? Are we going to take an airplane?"

"Well, not as far as China, but we will have to take an airplane. We are moving to a place called Cedarville, Iowa. I'm going to do work for a university near there."

"What kind of work? Can't you just do it here and mail it to them?"

"That would be nice, Elaine, but I have to be there to help them with a big project. They need me to tell them what to do. Just the way you need your teacher in school."

So Elaine had had to leave all her friends, and Pau-Pah, too, but at least Mei Lee got to move with them. Still it was awfully hard not to have anyone but Mei Lee to talk to. "Jeffrey and Kimiko, do you miss me like I miss you?" she said, half out loud.

In class, Ms. Bonovox announced, "We are going to begin a science project. We will study flying objects. You will all have a partner. Today we will go on a field trip to look at butterflies."

Elaine's partner was Mary Lewis Thorp. Elaine knew her name because when the Chow family moved to Cedarville, Mary Lewis's mother had brought a huge basket of fruit to the Chow family to welcome them. She was nice, but she talked a lot.

"Hi," Mary Lewis said, coming up to Elaine. "My name is Mary Lewis. Do you like butterflies?"

"Yes, but I don't like to catch them," Elaine said.

"Me neither. I would rather catch frogs

down at the creek. I wish they could fly. Then maybe we could study frogs instead of butterflies."

"I've never seen a real frog before," Elaine said. "Only in my science books and in the encyclopedia."

"You haven't?" Mary Lewis asked. "Well, maybe we can sneak off later and I'll show you a real one!"

But Ms. Bonovox had strict rules. She made everyone stay in a group on the field trip.

"Ms. Bonovox sure watches us like a hawk," Mary Lewis complained. "How does she do it? She's always wearing those dark sunglasses."

Elaine liked Ms. Bonovox. "Maybe she can't see without them?" she suggested.

"I think she wears them so they'll match her black outfits," Mary Lewis said. "I'm surprised she doesn't make us catch only black butterflies." Mary Lewis giggled.

"Oh, I kind of like this one with the yellow wing tips," Elaine said, going after it.

"Now remember," Ms. Bonovox said when they got back to the classroom, "we are to let these go after class. So don't even think about sticking them into a photo album or laminating them onto pins. We are only going to observe how they fly. Did you know that butterflies' wings are a lot like birds' wings? Dragonflies and ordinary houseflies move their wings much faster. The rapid motion causes the buzzing sound you hear."

"I think butterflies are a lot prettier than flies," said Kelleen. "I don't even know why we have flies. My cat Mork eats them all the time. Why do we have flies, Ms. Bonovox?"

"One time my cat ate a fly and threw up on my mom!" Harry Druze said.

"Harry, you're so gross!" Mary Lewis said, making a face.

Elaine thought, *He's sort of cute*. If she turned her head to the side, he looked a little like Jeffrey. Well, just a bit. She started to laugh at Harry, but the rest of the class was groaning.

"I think we have flies so frogs can eat them," Mary Lewis said.

"You've asked a good question, Kelleen," said Ms. Bonovox. "Class, I would like you to look that up in your science book tonight for homework." Everyone groaned again.

"Thanks a lot, Kelleen," Mary Lewis said.

"And for Monday I want you and your partner to bring in a flying object. I'll give you these few days and the weekend to think of something," Ms. Bonovox added.

"From nature, or man-made?" asked Harry.

"Either one. Be creative!"

"And don't you dare bring in something disgusting or I'll scream," Kelleen said.

"How about a frog, Ms. Bonovox?" Mary Lewis asked, waving her hand in the air.

"Mary Lewis, honestly, do frogs fly?" asked Ms. Bonovox.

"Well, no," Mary Lewis said.

"It seems you've answered your own question," the teacher said.

"I wonder if there is a way to make frogs fly," Mary Lewis whispered to Elaine. "Do you want to go down to the creek after school? I'll show you plenty of frogs, Elaine."

"Oh, yes," Elaine said, excitedly. She couldn't wait to see a creek filled with frogs.

"Mary Lewis and Elaine, please save your whispers until class is over," Ms. Bonovox said, peering over her glasses.

For the rest of the day Elaine had to struggle to keep from asking Mary Lewis more.

Elaine remembered what her grandmother had told her about making friends. "Friends are like flowers, Elaine," Pau-Pah said one day when Elaine was helping her grandmother plant *bok choy*, Chinese cabbage, in the garden. "You must be patient with them. It takes time for beautiful things to grow."

Elaine thought her grandmother was one of the smartest people she knew. Pau-Pah had already lived eight of Elaine's lives, and to Elaine that was a very long time.

Finally school was over, and Elaine and Mary Lewis were walking down to the creek. "Mary Lewis," Elaine asked, "how did you get your first name? I've had friends with different names, like Kimiko, and Mei Lee, my cat, but not one named Mary Lewis."

"I was named after a great-great-great-aunt who came here a long time ago from down South. Virginia, I think. I have another aunt named Mary Lewis. My family likes handing down that name for some reason." Mary Lewis shrugged. "It is kind of different, isn't it? I guess I'm pretty much an oddball around here."

"Well, me too," Elaine said. "My name is different, too."

"Elaine's not different," said Mary Lewis.

"Well, Elaine is only my English name. My parents named me that because it's the closest they could get to my Chinese name."

"Your Chinese name? What's that?" Mary Lewis asked curiously.

Elaine hesitated for a moment, then answered, "Oi Lai. Well, I guess it's not that close." Elaine laughed.

"Oi Lai, Oi Lai," Mary Lewis repeated. For an instant, Elaine thought Mary Lewis might make a face the way Kelleen did when she saw the fried rice. But instead, Mary Lewis asked, "Are you named after someone like I am?"

"Well, no. You see, when my mother was my age she lived in the mountains in China. Every day on her way to school she passed these flowers near her home. They were yellow orchids. When she came to this country she missed them so much she decided to name me after them. So my name really means orchid."

"Gosh, I wish I could be named after something I like," Mary Lewis said. "But I suppose I couldn't go around with a name like Frog Thorp."

"Mary Lewis, you're so funny." Elaine giggled.

"Oh, look, do you see there, Elaine! I think I see a frog!" Mary Lewis shouted, running down to the edge of the creek.

Elaine followed Mary Lewis to some rocks. "Where?" Elaine asked, eagerly straining to see a frog. Before she could take another step closer, Mary Lewis scooped one up into her hands. Elaine jumped back.

"Oh, don't be scared," Mary Lewis said,
holding out the struggling frog.

Elaine stuck a finger out to feel its skin. The frog blinked his eyes at her.

"They've got really sticky tongues," Mary Lewis said, holding the frog to her face. "Sometimes I pretend I'm a frog when I eat my cereal. But I have to do it when my mother's not looking. She said it isn't polite table manners."

Elaine laughed. "I would like to try that sometime!"

"It works the best with Froot Loops or Cheerios," Mary Lewis said, rolling her tongue out and back like a frog.

"How about rice?" Elaine asked.

"Sure, rice sticks to your tongue great, too!" Mary Lewis said.

Elaine smiled, and tried rolling her tongue. She was glad Mary Lewis hadn't asked her all about eating rice.

"Elaine, did you know some people eat frogs?" Mary Lewis asked. She set the creature on a rock. He scrambled away into the water.

"I eat fish," Elaine said, "but I don't think I could eat a frog."

"Me neither!" Mary Lewis declared.

Mary Lewis then showed Elaine some tadpoles swimming in the water, and how to skip rocks across the creek.

"Watch this, Elaine," Mary Lewis said, rubbing a flat rock on her skirt. She bent down low, and flipped the rock into the creek. Elaine watched the rock skip twice over the water.

"Do you want to try?" Mary Lewis asked. "You have to use a really flat rock." She handed Elaine a rock from the edge of the creek.

Elaine flung her rock out into the water, but it just sank.

"Naw, Elaine. You have to flip it out of your hand like this." Mary Lewis took a rock and showed Elaine.

"Like this?" Elaine picked up another flat rock and tried it again. Her rock skimmed across the water this time.

"Yeah, you did it!" yelled Mary Lewis, jumping up and down.

Elaine couldn't stop smiling. It felt like the time she first learned to blow a bubble with her gum. It took a whole week, but when Elaine could finally blow a bubble, she couldn't stop. Elaine didn't want to stop skipping rocks, either. Pretty soon, Mary Lewis and Elaine had skipped practically every flat rock they could find.

"Gosh, Elaine, I wish there was some way we could make a frog fly," sighed Mary Lewis as they started for home.

"Yeah. They turn into frogs from tadpoles. Too bad they can't become butterflies after that," Elaine said.

"Too bad we can't live in Disneyland either," said Mary Lewis.

"Well, I'll try really hard to think of a project tonight," Elaine said.

"Me too," agreed Mary Lewis.

Elaine couldn't wait to go home and tell her mother all about her new friend. Soon she was running.

"Mom, Mom," Elaine said, running into the house. Her mother was breaking string beans at the kitchen table.

"Mom, I met this girl at school today," Elaine said excitedly, coming into the kitchen. "She's real nice and taught me all about frogs."

"Slow down, Elaine," Mrs. Chow said. "Why don't you sit down? Do you want some water?"

"No," Elaine said, sitting down at the table. She wondered why everybody always thought you needed water when you got excited.

"What's her name?"

"Mary Lewis. She's the daughter of that Mrs. Thorp who came over with the fruit." Elaine started to eat the string beans out of the strainer.

"Elaine, stop it. We're going to have supper soon." Mrs. Chow moved the strainer out of her reach. "Unless you want to help me *bai* [break], then go outside and play.

"*Eiyah*," her mother suddenly said. "Where have you been in your shoes?"

Elaine looked at her shoes. She had forgotten to take them off before coming into the house. "We went down to the creek to look at frogs, Mother," Elaine said. It was always a rule to take your shoes off before entering.

"I better go play," Elaine said, getting up from the table. She had an idea: she wanted to try jumping like a frog.

Chapter 3

Instead of going outside, Elaine went into the den and, forgetting all about her mother's house rules, took the pillows off the couch and lined them up in a row on the floor. Then she crouched very low and jumped as high as she could, flinging her arms and legs out. She pounced down on the big pillows one after another, barely missing Mei Lee's tail. Mei Lee was having just as much fun darting back and forth around Elaine and the pillows.

Mrs. Chow heard strange thuds from the den and went back to find out what was going on. "Elaine, look what you've done to this room!"

"I'm a frog, Mother!" Elaine said, continuing to leap into the air and collapse back down onto the pillows.

"Tell me, Elaine, who did you like meeting better? Mary Lewis or the frogs?" Mrs. Chow asked, picking up a pillow each time Elaine jumped to the next one. "And you still have your shoes on! *Eiyah!* Go outside and jump where real frogs jump, Elaine. I don't want you to hit your head on the furniture like cousin Hwai-Hwai did when you were both jumping off the couch."

"Oh, Mom. We were just little kids then. We were airplanes!"

"So, she cracked her head open for being an airplane. What a silly watermelon head," Mrs. Chow said in Chinese.

Elaine started buzzing around like a jet.

"I don't understand you sometimes, Elaine. Now go outside until suppertime," Mrs. Chow said, pointing toward the door.

At the supper table, Elaine tried to sneak in some practice rolling her tongue in and out with rice on it.

"Elaine, what are you doing?" Mr. Chow asked.

Elaine looked up from her rice bowl, startled, with her tongue still curled. But she couldn't really talk like that. She uncurled her tongue and answered, "Eating like a frog."

"What?" Mr. Chow asked.

"Oh, Elaine met a girl in school today who's crazy about frogs. It's that nice Mrs. Thorp's daughter. Apparently she's been teaching Elaine all about frogs."

"Her name is Mary Lewis, Daddy," said Elaine.

"Well, do Mary Lewis's parents let her make

those faces at the dinner table?" Mr. Chow asked.

"No, she only does it when her mother's not looking."

"All I can say is, she must be awfully skinny. You will be too, Elaine, if you don't eat your food properly. Sit up straight."

"Oh, Daddy, I was just trying to see how frogs eat. Besides, I would rather have rice any day over flies and gnats."

"Elaine, I don't think this is table conversation," her mother said.

"Elaine, what else did you learn in school today besides eating like a frog?" Mr. Chow asked.

"Well, Ms. Bonovox—that's my teacher—" Elaine said, smiling, "has us studying flying objects in science class."

"Isn't she the teacher we saw who wears those dark glasses?" Mr. Chow asked.

"She told me she used to live in San Francisco, Daddy!"

"Really?" Mr. Chow asked, surprised.

"Yes, that's right. Mrs. Thorp mentioned something about her," said Mrs. Chow. "She's supposed to be some sort of artist. Everyone seems to think she's very creative with the children."

"Do you like Ms. Bonovox, Elaine?" asked Mr. Chow.

"Well, I do. Some of the kids think she's weird. But she's not! She's just—different. Ms. Bonovox wants us to bring in a flying object next week for our project in class."

"What sort of flying object?" Elaine's father asked.

"Well, Mary Lewis wanted to bring in a frog. But frogs don't fly. Can you help me think of a project?"

"Why don't you come down to my workshop after supper. Perhaps we can lay out some sort of project together," Mr. Chow said.

Now that Elaine's family lived in a bigger house, Mr. Chow had space for a workshop in the basement. He liked to build things. Most of all he loved to build kites.

When Mr. Chow went down to his workshop after supper, Elaine was already there. She was jumping all over the basement.

"Elaine, what are you doing now?" her father asked.

Elaine stumbled into the worktable and upset a bottle of glue. It fell on the floor. "Sorry, Daddy," she said, picking it up.

"Come here, Elaine. I think I have an idea for this flying project of yours."

"You do?" Elaine asked, getting all excited. "What?"

"Well, since you are so interested in frogs, why not make a frog into a kite? That way you could bring in a frog and also an object that flies."

"Gosh, I bet that's the best idea for a flying object anybody will come up with," Elaine said, beaming. "But Daddy, can you help us? I don't think either Mary Lewis or I know how to build a kite."

"I would be delighted to help build this best idea for a flying object," said Mr. Chow. And he gave his daughter a big hug.

The next morning Elaine ran almost the whole way to school. She saw Mary Lewis in the playground. "Mary Lewis, Mary Lewis!" she called, running across the wet grass. The morning dew was still visible, and by the time Elaine reached Mary Lewis her shoes were soaking wet.

"Hi, Elaine," Mary Lewis greeted her. "I tried all last night to think of something to bring in for our science project. But I couldn't think of anything good!"

Just then Kelleen walked up to Elaine and Mary Lewis. "Hi. What are you guys bringing in next week for your science project?"

"Well, we don't know yet," Mary Lewis said. Kelleen seemed to be waiting for them to ask her something.

"Well, in case you wanted to know, I'm bringing in a ladybug," Kelleen finally told them.

"Oh, that's nice," Elaine said.

"Yeah, well, I thought so, too." Kelleen smiled. "I suppose you still want to bring in a frog, Mary Lewis. Silly, frogs can't fly."

Elaine could tell Mary Lewis was trying awfully hard not to push Kelleen down or call her Stinky Pinky, her secret nickname.

"Oh, there's Melinda Pappajohn," Kelleen said. "I heard she was bringing in a bat! I should go and tell her about my ladybug, too."

"Boy, she makes me so mad sometimes," Mary Lewis said as Kelleen left. "I almost called her Stinky Pinky to her face!"

"Oh, never mind her, Mary Lewis. Listen, I have an idea," Elaine said.

"What?"

"Well, why *not* make a frog fly?"

"Just how are we supposed to do that, Elaine? Put a zillion fly wings on it?"

"Gross! No, we can't make a real frog fly, but we can make a frog into a kite," Elaine explained.

"But," Mary Lewis said, frowning and looking disappointed, "Elaine, I don't know how to make a kite. Do you?"

"Well, just a little bit, I do. But that doesn't matter. My father is going to help us. He builds kites as a hobby. He even can make one out of bamboo and rice paper. You know, all the stuff to make a real kite."

"Gee, Elaine, where are we going to get stuff like that to build a kite? I suppose I could have my mom take me to Target this weekend. They sell everything there."

"My dad already has it. You'll see."

"Really?" Mary Lewis said, her eyes widening.

"Really. Why don't you come over to my house on Saturday? My father can help us then."

"Wow, a frog that flies!" Mary Lewis grinned. "Won't Ms. Bonovox be surprised."

Chapter 4

Elaine was watching out of the window the next morning for Mary Lewis. She rode up the Chows' driveway at nine o'clock, on a green bike with a frog's-head horn on the handle-bars.

Elaine dashed out to the porch to greet her. "Hi, Mary Lewis!" she called, waving.

Elaine's mother came out of the house, too. "You must be Mary Lewis. Elaine hasn't stopped talking about you. She jumped all over the living room pretending to be a frog."

"Well, frogs are hot, Mrs. Chow." Mary Lewis laughed. "I hope some day to have my own frog farm. I'm going to call it The Mary Lewis Frog Farm."

"Sounds like a good name to me." Mrs. Chow smiled. "Would you girls like something to drink? How about some juice?"

"What's that you're drinking, Mrs. Chow?" Mary Lewis asked, peering into Mrs. Chow's cup.

"Tea."

"I always thought tea came in those little bags with the funny man wearing a skipper's hat. What are those little things floating around?"

"These are tea leaves, Mary Lewis." Mrs. Chow laughed. "Tea can also come like this. The tea leaves are packed inside a cannister. They're grown in my hometown in China, and then are shipped here. Come with me. I'll show you."

Mary Lewis and Elaine watched Mrs. Chow put some water in a teakettle to boil on the stove. Then she took a cannister from the shelf and put some tea leaves into a teapot.

"Mrs. Chow," Mary Lewis asked as Mrs. Chow poured the hot water into the teapot, "do you think I might have some tea instead of juice to drink?"

"Of course you may, Mary Lewis," she said, pouring tea for both girls.

Mary Lewis watched as a few tea leaves swirled into her cup.

"Oh, Mary Lewis, you've got a boyfriend," Mrs. Chow said.

"You mean that Sammy in the fourth grade? How did you know about him?"

Mrs. Chow laughed. "Whenever you get a stray tea leaf in your cup it means you have a boyfriend."

"Oh," Mary Lewis said, embarrassed.

After Mrs. Chow had given the girls their cups of tea, Elaine took Mary Lewis by the arm and pulled her down the stairs.

"Come on, Mary Lewis, my dad is waiting for us."

Mary Lewis was amazed by all the kites hanging up in the Chows' basement. "Wow, Elaine, did your father make all these kites?" she asked.

"Well, some of them my grandfather built. He taught my father to make kites, and his father taught him. It's a custom that's been handed down in my family."

"Gee, my mom's trying to teach me how to

knit, but I think learning how to build a kite is much more exciting. How long does it take to make one?"

"Well, it depends on what kind of kite," Elaine said. "I suppose the same way it is with knitting."

"I hope not," Mary Lewis said, crossing her arms. "Do you know it's taken my mom almost a whole year to knit me a sweater?"

Elaine laughed.

"Hello there, girls," said Mr. Chow, looking up from his worktable. He was busily twisting string around some wooden strips. "So you want to make a flying frog?"

"Oh, yes," Mary Lewis said, walking over to the table. "It's so nice of you to help, Mr. Chow. I don't know how to make a kite."

"I'm happy to help, Mary Lewis. Building kites is something I regard very highly. Kites were invented in China many years ago."

"They were?" asked Mary Lewis.

"Hmm, I'd say almost two thousand years ago," said Mr. Chow.

"Wow, that's older than my mother's tea set!

The one Great-Aunt Mary Lewis from Virginia gave her. That's the oldest thing I've ever known."

"Well, China's a very old country," remarked Mr. Chow.

"Just how did they come to make the kite, Dad?" Elaine asked her father.

"Yeah, I always thought Benjamin Franklin invented the kite," Mary Lewis said.

"Oh no. There are a lot of stories about how the kite helped Benjamin Franklin experiment with electricity," Mr. Chow said. "But originally, kites were made to help warriors in battle.

"You see, many years ago—even before your Great-Aunt Mary Lewis's tea set," Mr. Chow began, "a general used the first kites to figure out how far away his enemy's fortress was. The wind carried the kite to the fortress, and then the general pulled it back and measured the string. The general then knew how long to make the tunnels leading right up to the enemy fortress. The enemy had no idea what this flying object was."

"Gosh," said Mary Lewis. "Maybe the people who saw the kites were scared."

"Well, Mary Lewis, we think that is exactly what happened to the villagers who saw the strange flying objects. Nobody knew what they were, so people said they were magical spirits or messages from the gods."

"Yeah, except for the clever general, and his soldiers!" Elaine said firmly.

Mr. Chow continued his story. "As kites became more popular, they were used for more than just fighting battles. People used them for festivals, and they began to say that kites in different shapes had different meanings. Animal kites have always meant something special. For instance, cranes and turtles represent long life. Some were said to give good luck, and others were used to frighten evil spirits away."

"Did they ever use frogs, Mr. Chow?" Mary Lewis asked.

"A frog," mused Mr. Chow. "Hmm. I don't know. I suppose you girls will have to think up your own meaning for a frog kite." Mr. Chow then held up the wooden strips he had been tying together with string.

"Gosh, it really looks like a frog," Mary Lewis said, amazed.

"But what can we do, Dad?" Elaine asked.

"Yes, we have to help or it won't be our project," Mary Lewis said.

"Okay. Why don't you take some of this rice paper and put some green paint on it. You girls know what frogs look like; I don't think that should be any problem for you!"

Elaine and Mary Lewis busily went to work painting the rice paper with watercolors. Elaine even found some gold sequins, and they began pasting those all over the paper, too.

"Gosh, Elaine, what do you suppose a frog kite would mean?" Mary Lewis asked her. She had gotten a gold sequin stuck to her thumb, and she was trying to pull it off.

"How are you two doing?" Mr. Chow asked. "Looks like you've gotten more sequins on yourselves than on the frog."

"It's hard, Daddy." Elaine frowned. "The glue dries too fast for us." She began picking sequins off her sweatshirt.

"Well, that's pretty good," Mr. Chow said, admiring the work Elaine and Mary Lewis had done with the rice paper. "I think we can put this rice paper on the frog's body now."

"We can?" Mary Lewis asked. "How are we going to do that?"

"Carefully!" Mr. Chow laughed. "It takes a

lot of glue, and I wouldn't want to send you home all sticky like a caramel apple, Mary Lewis."

The girls took the colored rice paper and pasted it on the frog's body. It was deep, dark green with some yellow streamers on the side. Elaine and Mary Lewis drew in the eyes with black crayon. They used two Ping-Pong balls for the eyeballs.

"I do think that's the best-looking kite in Iowa," said Mr. Chow. "Wouldn't you agree?"

Elaine and Mary Lewis beamed.

"I can't wait to bring it to school on Monday. Can we fly it yet?" Mary Lewis asked.

Mr. Chow shook his head. "It's still a bit wet. But I think by Monday it will be just fine."

"Fantastic," Elaine said excitedly. "Won't Ms. Bonovox be pleased."

"What do you mean, Ms. Bonovox?" said Mary Lewis. "*I'm* proud."

Early Monday morning, Mary Lewis arrived at Elaine's to help carry the kite. They had put it in a plastic garbage bag to keep it a surprise.

When they set the garbage bag upon the project table, the whole class came buzzing around Elaine and Mary Lewis.

"What is it?" Harry asked. "I'll tell you what mine is if you tell me what yours is. I brought in a moth."

"Well, it's a—" began Elaine. Mary Lewis nudged her to be quiet.

"No, Harry, it's a surprise. You'll see," Mary Lewis said.

"It looks like our Christmas tree stuck in a garbage bag after New Year's Day," Kelleen said.

Mary Lewis gave Kelleen a dead stare. Kelleen quickly moved away from the table.

"Okay, class, that's enough. Please return to your seats," Ms. Bonovox said.

"Who would like to go first with their science project?" she asked.

A few children raised their hands, and Ms. Bonovox started picking students in the front.

"I was waving my hand as high as I could," Mary Lewis said to Elaine, disappointed.

"That's okay, Mary Lewis, we can wait," Elaine said.

Harry was the next to be chosen. "I caught this moth right outside my house." Harry held up his jar with the gray moth fluttering in it. "It made a cocoon right on our tree in the front yard. There used to be a bunch of them, but my mom knocked all the other cocoons down."

"Why did your mom do that, Harry?" asked a boy who sat next to Elaine.

"She said she didn't want them flying into the house every time I opened the door. My mom said they would eat my sweaters and socks. Why would they do that, Ms. Bonovox? I mean, what happens when they have to go to the bathroom?"

"Harry, that's enough for now," Ms. Bonovox said. Then she saw Mary Lewis's hand waving, and sighed. "All right, Mary Lewis, you can be next. You have had your arm up and down so much you could lead us in gym class today."

"Oh, goody. Do you want to see a frog fly, Ms. Bonovox?"

"If it's possible."

"Hey, Ms. Bonovox, I'm Mary Lewis Thorp, and anything is possible for me!"

The kids eagerly circled around the mystery

in the plastic garbage bag. Elaine and Mary
Lewis slowly and carefully removed the cover-
ing from the kite. The class oohed and aahed.

"Hey," Kelleen said. "That doesn't look anything like an old Christmas tree. It looks like a
kite. A *frog kite!*"

"Does it fly?" someone asked.

"Of course it does, silly," Mary Lewis said. "Elaine's father helped us build it. Did you know that kites came from China over two thousand years ago?"

"Hey, Mary Lewis, that's older than your great-aunt's tea set," Harry said.

"Oh, I know, and I used to think that was really old. Did you know kites have special meanings?"

"Elaine, can you tell us what?" Ms. Bonovox asked.

"Well, a dragon kite means prosperity for good fishing," Elaine explained.

"What?" Kelleen asked, confused.

"You know, that you will catch a lot of fish!"

"So what about a frog?" asked Harry.

"I think a frog means . . ." Mary Lewis said, looking at Elaine, ". . . friendship! Isn't that right, Elaine?"

"Oh, yes, a frog kite means friendship," Elaine said, smiling happily.

"How literally fascinating," said Ms. Bonovox. She was smiling too. "Class, wouldn't you agree?"

After they sat down again, Elaine couldn't help feeling good and warm inside. Suddenly, her friends Jeffrey, Kimiko, and Sherry in San Francisco didn't seem so far away. Elaine could see them smiling through her new friends in the classroom.

"Elaine, we were a big hit," Mary Lewis said to Elaine as the second bell rang for recess.

Everybody was soon swarming around the cubbyholes for their jackets to go outside.

"Yeah. I told my father it was the best idea for a flying object." Elaine grinned, putting on her jacket.

"You were right," Mary Lewis said, reaching into her cubbyhole for her jacket, too.

Suddenly Elaine noticed a rope on the top shelf of Mary Lewis's cubbyhole.

"Hey, Mary Lewis," Elaine asked, getting excited. "Is that a jump rope?"

"Yeah," Mary Lewis said, pulling it out to show Elaine.

"Gee, Mary Lewis, I didn't know you liked to jump rope," Elaine said. "Look, see, sometimes I carry my jump rope in my pocket for good luck." Elaine struggled with her coat pocket to show Mary Lewis her jump rope.

"Wow," Mary Lewis said. "You must really like to jump rope!"

"All the way to Mexico!" Elaine said.

"Hey, I know that one!" Mary Lewis laughed.

Elaine couldn't wait to get to the playground to jump rope.

"How about this one, Elaine, do you know this one?" Mary Lewis asked as they were walking outside. "Teddy bear, teddy bear . . ." she began.

". . . sitting in a golden chair!" Elaine chanted, joining in.

"Thinks he is a millionaire!" They finished together.

"Hey, what are you guys doing?" Kelleen asked. Kelleen was sitting on the ground drawing a game of hopscotch on the sidewalk. Mary

Lewis and Elaine had walked right into one of her neatly chalked pink squares.

"We're going to jump rope. Do you want to jump rope with us, Kelleen?" asked Elaine.

"I just got a new jump rope yesterday at Target. It's pink. Now it matches my lunch box. It's in my cubbyhole, though."

"Hey, Elaine," said Harry, coming up to them just then. "Would you like to go look for some worms?"

"Ugh," Mary Lewis said, making a face.

"Harry, are you going to be gross again?" asked Kelleen. "I'll scream. I swear I will."

"Well, gee, Harry," Elaine said. "We're going to jump rope. Would you like to jump rope, too?"

"That's for girls," Harry said.

"It is not," Mary Lewis said. "Don't you know boxers jump rope, Harry?"

"Okay," Harry said, "but can't I just hold the end of the rope?"

"I'll hold the other end," Kelleen said.

"Okay," Elaine said. When they all got to the playground, Elaine and Mary Lewis tied their ropes together. Harry and Kelleen started swinging.

Mary Lewis jumped in first.
"I like coffee,
"I like tea . . ." she began to sing.
"I would like my friend Elaine
"to jump with me!"
And Elaine jumped in.